WILDFLOWER

ONE

WILD Duet

AN ASHFORD FAMILY NOVEL

D.M. DAVIS

WILDFLOWER by D.M. Davis
Published by D.M. Davis

ISBN: 979-8-9869509-1-4

www.dmckdavis.com
Cover Design by D.M. Davis
Cover Photo by Depositphotos
Editing by Tamara Mataya
Proofreading by Mountains Wanted Publishing & Indie Author Services
Formatting by Champagne Book Design

This book is a work of fiction. Names, characters, places, and incidents are either the product of the author's imagination or are used fictitiously.

This story contains mature themes, strong language, and sexual situations. It is intended for adult readers.

ABOUT THIS BOOK

D.M. Davis' **WILDFLOWER** is a heartwarming, secret crush, first responder, steamy contemporary romance between a firefighter and a local flower shop owner.

She's a five-alarm fire I've no wish to extinguish.

She pushes all my buttons, strikes me in just the right way.

From her pale green gaze as she nervously brushes her wavy locks from her face, to the stammer in her flustered responses—I can't get enough.

I brave fires for a living, yet this connection is so flammable, I'm afraid to touch it.

Afraid to mess it up.

Afraid to get burned.

When destiny has her in need of help, I'm there.

She gives me an inch. I'm stealing a mile.

Taking her for the ride of our lives.

Only fate has other plans, forcing me to make an impossible life or death decision I'm afraid she can never forgive.

WILD Duet is the beginning of D.M. Davis' *Ashford Family* series.

Disclaimer

This is a work of fiction, straight from my heart. Please extend grace to any inaccuracies. While trying to honor the brave men and women who protect us from such tragedies, I took some creative liberties for the sake of the story. In no way did I meant any disrespect to these real-life heroes and the people who love them.

DEDICATION

For the men and women who run toward the fire.
Into chaos and danger.
Who are brave despite their fear.
For saying *yes*, when most say *no*.
I honor you as best I can with my words.

WILDFLOWER

CHAPTER 1

THE BELL CHIMES AND HEAVY BOOTS LAND on the linoleum floor. I freeze, my back to the door, Stacy at the counter, and a catch in my breath when recognition rings through my body.

It's *him*.

It's Tuesday. Seven-thirty on the dot. Like clockwork.

The earth shifts whenever he steps into my store, Daisy's Blooming Flower Shoppe. I fight for footing, for grace, for my next breath. Every. Dang. Time.

It's not his size that has my world trembling—though he is built like a giant sequoia—it's the zing up my spine, the intensity of his stare, and the gruff in his voice, like he's been chewing bark for breakfast.

"Good morning," Stacy's gleeful greeting has me wanting to shake my head in disbelief.

He won't respond, no matter how hard she tries. He ignores her while his heated gaze drills into my back.

The silence pounds in my ears. If it weren't for the soft, masterful strumming of Trace Bundy's acoustic rendition of Pachelbel's *Canon*, all we'd hear is my struggle to breathe.

"Um, Boss?"

Have pity on her by jumping in to save her from his intensity, or give myself just another second to believe he's really here to see me?

Yeah, like the flowers he buys every Tuesday aren't proof enough he's got someone he dotes on. Lucky girl.

He only likes to deal with me because I was the one to wait on him the first time he came in early last year. It's hard to believe it's been over a year of his weekly visits. We're not even technically open, except for deliveries and those early starters who can't wait until the eight o'clock hour.

A year. I've been crushing on the silent sequoia firefighter for *nearly* a year. Or maybe over a year. Honestly, I think he's been *crushing* me since our first encounter. His size and voice drew me in, but it was his own-the-room, single-minded focus that keeps me frozen, basking in his every word, glance, and gruff response. I'm a Reidaholic. I can't get enough. I'm drunk on him, and I've never even had a taste.

"Yep. Just a sec." Casual, right? I don't sound like I'm choking on air, trembling in my… I look down. He's got me so rattled I can't even remember which of my cute sneakers I have on today. Lavender chucks. They match my flowy skirt.

If I could be barefoot, I would. Sandals are my next choice, but working in a shop where things drop and glass breaks—I discovered the hard way—closed-toe shoes are the way to go. Plus, it's cold, especially in the fridge.

Have I stalled enough? Am I ready to accept the fact that he's here to buy flowers for the woman in his life?

Yeah, the answer to that is *no*.

Why can't I find someone like him? Because I don't want someone *like* him. I want *him*.

A smile slips free when I turn to find him admiring a decorative vase of roses waiting for pick-up, rubbing the red ribbon between his meaty fingers.

"Good morning, Reid." There. I sounded like an adulting business owner and not a heartsore, unrequited sad sack. I consider that my win for the day.

That is until his eyes ping to mine and hold. "Mornin', Flower."

Darn that soulful voice of his. Honey, whiskey, and crooning love songs are all I think of when he speaks. And when he calls me—

"You doin' okay?" He moves in, towering over me, making me feel small and petite, though I'm average in every way.

"I… yeah…" I clear my throat and settle on, "Yes. You?"

My fluster tips his lips and shines in his gentle eyes. He studies me as if my answer influences his day. "I'm good, Daisy."

He's always good. Even on the days he spent most of his

night fighting fires, rescuing people from car accidents, or multiple other disasters that can change the course of someone's life—he's always *good*.

"I made a new drink." I delay the inevitable—asking what flowers he wants for his girl.

"Yeah?" His curious brows rise. "Give me a taste." He reaches over, swiping the tumbler with my logo on it, and takes a deep drink. I try not to drool over his bulging biceps and bobbing Adam's apple as he swallows. His eyes narrow as he sets the cup down. "You made this?"

"Y-yes." Does he hate it?

"It's really good. Damn good."

Goosebumps break out along my arms at his praise. I push the tumbler his direction. "Take it if you'd like."

"Naw, it's yours."

"I have more." I don't tell him I made this smoothie, like all the others these past months, just for him. I don't drink coffee. He noticed, took an interest in my morning smoothies, and somehow it's become a thing we share. I like to experiment and try to surprise him.

"Thanks." His hand practically swallows the tumbler. "What's in this one?"

"Wild berries, peaches, yogurt, spinach, honey, cinnamon, and some other stuff to make it extra healthy."

"You should sell these, make a killing."

I laugh. Customers don't come in here to drink my concoctions. They come for flowers, not flower petal-infused overpriced beverages. It's not the first time we've had this discussion.

I'm spread thin. My drinks are something I do for me—and him. Taking on another To Do is not high on my list of *To Dos*. Speaking of… I reluctantly ask the inevitable, "What'll it be to-day?" that'll burst this bubble and send us both back to work.

His brow pinches, but he nods.

He glances at the display case of premade arrangements and then to the other one with buckets of flowers *waiting* to be made into beautiful bouquets. Hands in his pockets, his gaze slides to my blouse and up to my face. The warmth in his brown eyes makes me feel like I'm being swallowed by quicksand an inch at a time.

"Purple."

The color of my blouse. He wants to give his girl flowers inspired by me? I'm not sure how I feel about that.

He nods. "Purple, Daisy."

"Okay." I get to work assembling a mix of lavender and purple roses, alstroemeria, carnations, matsumoto asters, snapdragons, bells of Ireland, huckleberry, green button spray chrysanthemums, and lemon leaf.

By the time I'm done, he's finished the smoothie and set the tumbler on the counter with his debit card beside it. "Add in a nice tip," he insists even though I never do.

How awkward is it for me to figure out how much *extra* I'm worth? If he specified a dollar amount, I'd maybe do it and give it to Stacy. But it feels like he wants me to have it, and so the whole thing doesn't feel right. I enjoy his visits, not for the monetary value but because I wish he came in just to see me.

"How 'bout you over-tip the next person instead?" Do I

sound ungrateful? "These flowers are enough. Besides, I threw in some ranunculus, which has been hard to find lately."

He grumbles his response, barely eyeing the bundle as I hand it over with his card and receipt before he walks away.

Except I have to hide my sad expression when, flowers in hand, he stops at the door, turning to face me. "You coming to the picnic on Saturday?"

"Everyone has the day off to attend." I don't tell him I'm staying behind to man the store. Though, I doubt we'll have much business, given it's an annual event put on by the city and pretty popular with the locals.

"Maybe I'll see you there."

Not unless you're coming here. "Maybe," I offer instead.

His gaze lingers a moment more before he turns with a, "See you later, Flower."

"See you," I whisper, leaning against the counter and letting out a deep breath, ignoring Stacy's smirk as she steps from the back, making her way to the front door, watching him leave.

Something I never have the heart to do. I prefer him entering as opposed to leaving.

CHAPTER 2

"DID YOU FIND YOUR BALLS THIS morning?" Jake slaps my back in greeting as he heads for the coffee.

"Apparently not. You miss the mope in his step? Our gentle giant can't seem to pull the trigger," Damon razes.

Gentle giant. They're mistaking quiet for gentle. Besides, I'm not feeling all that gentle at the moment. I wouldn't mind ripping one or two of their heads off. It'd make a mess, but I'm pretty sure I'd feel better.

"Damn, boy. You'd better step it up before some asshole takes her right out from under your nose." Jake sips his coffee, eyeing me over his steaming mug.

I focus on cooking the scrambled eggs, giving these hens something to cluck about besides my love life—or lack of one. They don't know my mom's been secretly trying to set us up for months, under the guise of a blind date, only Daisy isn't biting. I'd been working on my girl long before Mom starting talking me up. I've asked her to stop, but she's convinced she's making headway. I doubt it.

Daisy isn't a blind date kind of girl.

Could she have a boyfriend I don't know about?

Is she into women? Nah, she gets too flustered around me to not be into guys.

Just not interested? Her eyes tell me she is, even if she doesn't want to be.

My Flower doesn't know it's my mom she's befriended. They met at the Flower Mart and became friendly. Daisy is easy like that, open, welcoming, gentle, but skittish like a doe, easily spooked.

I pull the biscuits out of the oven, drop them next to the tray of bacon, turn off the stove, and ring the bell, barking, "Breakfast!"

The low murmur turns into a dull roar as the guys stomp in, ready to fill their bellies. Plates and utensils clang. Coffee, juice, and milk are passed around until everyone is settled. Judge says a quick prayer before we dig in.

My brothers, Galant and Turner, make plates and sit across from me, their eyes never leaving their food as they begin to inhale it.

"Any news on the wildfires?" Michael asks from the other end, his mouth stuffed with a whole biscuit.

Silence fills the room as every ear perks up to hear the answer.

It's the time of year when wildfires wreak havoc. They devastate the land, and if we can't stop or divert them, they consume homes, businesses, and sometimes lives. It's brutal hours and punishing calls. Gregary, my third brother, only a year older than me, is a smokejumper based in Redding. When needed, we help out, but the last we heard, they're still a ways out from our territory.

"Last report said the fire is still above the Bluff." Red, our captain, scans the room, his fork perched near his mouth. "It's business as usual, gentlemen." He takes his bite, looks at a rookie then adds, "Until it's not."

"Copy," and "Understood," and grumbles spread around the table.

We've been here before. It's not our first rodeo. I've been a firefighter for five years, like my brothers, my dad, and my grandfather.

It's in my blood, sweat, and tears. It's what I know.

Only once in my years of service have we not been called to combat the wildfires as they start or burn near our town and neighboring cities. I'm hoping we have another exception year. Though, if we get too much rain, we could be fighting floods and landslides. Not a great alternative. It'd be nice to have a year without any major catastrophes to fight, without chancing the loss of more firefighters, civilians, and wildlife.

Something in me is telling me to stay right where I am.

It's not a *don't go, don't fight the fires because something bad will happen if you do* feeling. It's a gut-binding *stay right where you are because your presence is needed here* feeling.

Flower.

Is she my reason? My pull to stay?

When hours pass emergency-free, my duties are done for the day, and the twist in my gut still hasn't eased. I get the okay from my supervisor to leave a few hours early. On my Harley Dyna Wide Glide, it only takes a handful of minutes till I'm speeding off and pulling up to the curb in front of Daisy's shop.

The door chimes as I enter, and some young guy peeks from the back room, hesitates, then steps into the front of the store. "Welcome to Daisy's Blooming Flower Shoppe. How can I help you?" His smile is too big. Too eager. Too nervous.

"Where's Daisy?" I can't help the steel in my tone. I'm not much of a people person. I'm not usually here at this time of day, but I've never seen this guy. He looks like a weasel, edgy and unreliable. He's not good enough for my Flower. I eye his nametag. *Mark.* At least I know it's a professional relationship. He works for her.

"She... uh—" He thumbs over his shoulder.

"She's in the basement." The blonde who usually covers the front of the shop moves into view with professionally unsettling information.

Buildings from this era are cute and have great architectural elements, but most of them in this old neighborhood need work. I've fought too many electrical fires and rescues from fallen walls during reconstruction to know these old buildings are mostly trouble. Nothing good can come from being in the basement.

I arch a brow, wanting details from the blonde mouse.

"Come on," she sighs, trotting to keep up as I close the space between me and my Flower. She points to the door in the back of the shop. "It's been a while. She told us to watch the place till she got back."

I could ask a hundred questions, but none of them matter, and none would get me downstairs any faster. Opening the door, the faint sound of running water greets me just as the cool blast of musty basement fills my nostrils. Unless she's doing laundry or washing something, running water is not a good sign.

"Daisy?"

"Oh, thank God." Her sigh of relief floods me with worry. "Don't let the door shut!"

When it starts to close on its own, I slap my palm against it, looking back at the blonde mouse. "Get something to prop the door open."

"On it." She disappears from view, coming back with a chair.

Daisy never should have come down here by herself, and with the door shut behind her. If she needed help, no one would have heard her.

Moving down the steps, I crouch down to see below the over-hang before I make it to the bottom.

"Reid, is that you?"

I progress quickly, but my foot nearly disappears into the water as I step off the last rung. "Jesus, Daisy." I find my girl across the room, soaking wet, holding on to an overhead pipe as it sprays water around her fist and all over her.

"I couldn't get out. I couldn't stop it." Her quivering voice sets me more on edge.

I need to get her out of here, make sure she's okay. I glance around, finding some rags and what looks to be an old smock to wrap around the pipe till I get the water shut off.

"My phone didn't work down here. And then I—"

"I got you." I squeeze in next to her, doing a visual examination, and clench when I spot blood on the other side of her face. "Let's get this water off and you outta here. Okay, Flower?"

"Yeah, okay." She nods, her chin trembling, looking all kinds of vulnerable in her drenched flowered overalls and white blouse—not what she was wearing earlier—hair plastered to her head, and those big doe eyes of hers taking me in. Even soaking wet, she's sexy as fuck. I have to pry her pretty hands off the pipe.

"I got you," I restate in case she didn't hear me the first time or comprehend my meaning: *I'm not letting anything bad happen to you.*

CHAPTER 3

SHAKING AND FULL OF RELIEF, I SINK INTO Reid's hold as he carries me upstairs, whispering, "I got you," into my hair.

Relief isn't a strong enough word to convey how I felt the moment Reid appeared on the basement stairs, his achingly soothing voice shattering my resolve. To be honest, it began the moment I heard big feet stomping their way closer above my head. It'd been hours, maybe longer, maybe less, water rising past my ankles despite trying to keep it at bay with my hands against the burst pipe. With the basement door locked or stuck, I had to choose between trying to stop the water or banging and screaming until Stacy or Mark heard me.

In hindsight, banging down the door probably would have been the smarter choice.

I'd come down to do laundry when I noticed the leaky pipe. I tried to tighten the bolt, holding the metal thingy around the pipe, but that's when it all blew up in my face. Literally. The bolt I'd been trying to tighten flew off, hitting me in the head, leaving a cut I didn't even know was bleeding until Reid swiped at my face, his hand coming away bloodied.

Barely winded, he sets me in a chair, grabs some paper towels and holds the wad against my head, his eyes brimming with worry. "Do you think you can hold it steady while I turn off the water?"

Though shaking like I took a mid-winter ice bath, I manage to replace his hand with mine, keeping steady pressure. "Thank you."

He smiles, pulling his phone out. "I'll be right back." He steps outside, speaking to whoever he called as he disappears.

"I'm so sorry. I should have checked on you—" Stacy wraps an old blanket I keep in the shop over my shoulders.

"It's okay."

"—I got distracted with the delivery orders."

I grip her hand, garnering her eyes. "It's okay. I'm okay. I should have propped the door open. I forgot about the faulty lock."

"He's coming." Mark jumps back and scurries toward us seconds before Reid stomps inside glowering, then continues to back away when Reid's destination appears to be me.

I'd laugh if I wasn't caught in the heated gaze of the giant sequoia moving ever closer. He brushes the hair from my face. "Water's off. My brothers are coming to fix the leak. You need to call the owner and let him know what's going on." When I only nod, he kneels in front of me, his hands resting on the chair's edge. "You doin' okay?"

Teeth chattering, I manage a simple, "Cold, but better."

"Hmm." He eyes my head. "Need to get you dried off and cleaned up, but it's kinda hard without water."

"I'll just go—" I stand but get lightheaded. "Whoa."

"Not so fast." Reid grips my hips, holding me steady as he rises to his feet and sweeps me in his arms, cradled against his chest again. Not complaining. "Where?"

"Out back." Stacy rushes toward the back door, pointing. "The stairs."

Reid comes to a stop outside, frowns between me and the wrought iron stairs that lead to the upstairs apartment. "You live above your shop?"

"Yeah."

"Keys!" Stacy runs inside, returning a second later with my purse.

"Thanks. I'll be back in a few."

"No, she won't," Reid's gruff reply doesn't leave much room for arguing.

I will. I just need to dry off, stop shaking, and get my feet under me. Literally. "You don't need to carry me."

"Humph." He climbs the stairs like carrying me is nothing. Given his size and his job, it probably is.

He does set me on my feet to unlock the door, then escorts me inside with a hand on by back. "No alarm?"

15

"No. I put in one for the shop, but I can't afford to monitor up here too."

His scowl only grows.

"You don't need to wait. I'll be down in a few—"

"You have bottled water? Tea?" He moves to the kitchen, opening a cabinet. "Hot chocolate." He glances over his shoulder. "That'll do."

"Water is in the refrigerator. And milk." I know some people like to make hot chocolate with milk. I grew up with water. It was cheaper and fewer calories. I don't care which he uses, I just need something warm.

He nods, pausing his movements when I only stand there watching him in my small space, looking like a bull in a China shop but moving like a gazelle on the open plains. "You need help, Flower?" His assessing gaze has me blushing.

I swallow past the want in my throat and murmur, "Uh, no." I stop when I'm on the other side of the bar, eyeing him through the cutout in the wall. "If I'd said yes, what would that look like?" I can't believe I'm actually asking.

His brows rise in surprise and settle lower when he leans across the counter, his jaw clenching and unclenching. His arms stretch out over the bar between us, his fingers able to touch me if I only move a few inches closer. "It'd look like me setting you on the bathroom counter, stripping you bare, examining every inch to be sure you're truly okay. Then drying you off. Doctoring your cut or anything else that needs attention. Helping you get dressed, probably in something fresh and toasty from the dryer.

Giving you a warm drink, and holding you till you stopped shaking and your teeth stopped chattering."

Jesus, help me. "Oh. Wow."

He leans closer, his fingers reaching to sweep a few wet hairs from my eyes. "You want that, Daisy?"

Oh God, do I. "I, uh, think I can manage."

He has a girlfriend. Doesn't he?

"Holler if you change your mind." He winks and pulls away, unraveling from the tight-fitting space, coming to his full height, his face barely visible under the upper cabinet. He cocks his head when I don't move, stuck staring at him, trying to figure him out. "Change your mind already?"

"Nope," I squeak and hurry to my room, the sound of his laughter trailing me.

I leave my Flower dry, tummy full of hot chocolate and ramen I found in the pantry, and asleep on her couch, wrapped in a big throw to keep her toasty, given the icepack I insisted she leave on her head till she dozed off.

Downstairs, I find my brothers working to fix the pipe while a pump pulls the water out of the basement. Another issue is why the drain in the basement isn't pulling the water out in the first place.

"What can I do to help?" I hand them both a bottled water from Daisy's fridge.

"You can get me Stacy's number," Turner, my second-to-oldest brother, requests as he solders the last of the new piping into place.

I glance at Galant, who only shrugs, not having a clue. So I ask, "Who's Stacy?"

Turner pivots, a brow raised. "Seriously? There are other women in the world besides your *Flower*."

"Watch it," I growl, not appreciating his tone.

"Easy." Galant presses his hand to my chest, stopping my advance, but speaks to my asshole brother, "Stop poking the bear. You know how he feels." He drops his hand when I step off. "Besides, he just found her locked in the basement alone with a broken water pipe threatening to drown her before she bled out from a head wound. Have some sympathy."

Turner punches out a breath, an apology in his eyes before he even opens his mouth. "Yeah, sorry. That had to be scary. Stacy, the blonde." He laughs. "Her other employee. Not the dude."

Weasel. "Got it. Nah, you're on your own on that one. Don't play if you've no intention of sticking around and being decent. I don't need your sex life ruining my chances with Daisy."

"God knows it won't be *your* sex life getting in the way." Turner has Galant laughing too.

"I'm selective who I spend my time with."

"You're so picky, you're celibate and you don't even realize it," Galant chimes in.

Oh, I realize it. My right hand can attest to that, not that I'd tell these assholes. "Like you're any better." I don't know the last time I saw Galant with a girl, or remember him even talking one up.

"Yeah!" Turner starts putting his tools away. "Y'all are gonna dry up like a bunch of old men if you don't use the gifts God gave you."

"Whatever." Galant points at me. "*You* need to figure this shit out. Ask her out or stop moping around about her."

"I know. She's just—"

"She's a beautiful woman who'd appreciate a gentle giant like you pining over her. Trust me. Girls eat it up." Turner acts like he's a love connoisseur. He doesn't know any more about it than we do. He's never had a serious girlfriend. He's tagging one-night stands like he's going for a trophy.

"I don't want to push Daisy if she's not ready."

"You've known her for over a year, Reid. It's time." Galant squeezes my shoulder, ever the oldest, protective brother. His furrowed brow punctuates his words. "Now, back to the matter at hand. The leak should be fixed. We installed all new pipe and fittings." He nods to Turner, who heads upstairs. "We'll test it out. Be sure there are no more leaks, but I got to be honest, man, who knows what's in these walls. Let's just hope when Turner turns the water on, the walls don't come crumbling down around us."

"Let's hope not. The landlord hasn't returned her calls. He's been ghosting her for weeks." I'll give him a few days to respond, then give the man a visit. Maybe seeing a man in uniform will have him considering the error of his ways.

"I trust you'll help her out with that."

"Of course." No doubt.

After testing the water lines held up, and I help pack their gear, leaving the pump running till all the water is gone, I thank Stacy and Mark for their help, and head back to my girl.

Not your girl.

I'm working on it. If I have way, she'll be mine by morning.

CHAPTER 4

MY BEDROOM COMES INTO FOCUS SLOWLY, the feeling of losing something—someone—lingering as I blink in the morning light. I groan as I stretch. My arms and legs are sore from standing on tip toe holding on to the water pipe for so long yesterday.

Yesterday?

I sit up in a panic and grip my head as it throbs in protest.

Yesterday?

Can it be morning? I'm in my bed, but I think I was on the couch.

I rip off the covers. T-shirt and panties. No yoga pants.

Think.

I close my eyes and take a few cleansing breaths.

I was on the couch with Reid. I was sleepy after the yummy hot chocolate and soup. I guess I fell asleep.

Did he carry me to bed? Did he take off my pants and socks? I cup my breast. Bra. I still have my bra on. Though, I'm a little disappointed I do.

Slowly I stand, gripping the post at the end of my bed where I find my pants slung over the corner. I slip them on and visit the bathroom before venturing to the kitchen for coffee, or maybe more hot chocolate.

I freeze at the sight of Reid in my kitchen, sipping coffee and flipping pancakes. His gaze lifts to me, his cup still at his mouth as his eyes rake over me from my bare feet to my disastrous mess of hair I clipped up moments ago.

"Morning, Flower. How you feelin'?"

Memories of a hard body and strong arms holding me infiltrate my mind. "Did you sleep with me last night?"

His smile is dangerously panty-dropping handsome. "You insisted when I tried to leave, so I did." He comes around the breakfast bar to stop in front of me. He hands me his cup of coffee. "I needed to be sure you were okay, anyhow. Didn't have any ill effects from the bump on the head and near hypothermia I found you in."

I take a long drink and sigh into his cup. "Thank you. I needed that."

"Hungry?"

"Starved."

He nods to the bar stools. "Sit. I'll make you a plate."

Wow. He saved me. Stayed with me. And made me breakfast. "Can I keep you?" I joke as I sit and take another sip of coffee, just sweet enough to satisfy.

"That depends." He slides a plate loaded with three pancakes, eggs, and bacon my direction.

"I didn't have the fixings for this." I eye my plate and him on repeat.

"I had a few groceries delivered." He slides onto the stool beside me. It creaks from his impressive size.

"Like I said, can I keep you?" I drizzle warm maple syrup over the pancakes and bacon.

"It still depends," he replies, his eyes on me as I focus on my food.

I'm not usually this brave. I was partially kidding, mostly hoping. I'm normally so nervous around him, but this feels different—he's different.

"I don't think your girlfriend would share you." Let's see what he says to—oh wow. I nearly die when I taste his pancakes. "Ohmygod! I could eat these every day." I'm used to my morning protein shakes, not real food, particularly sweet breakfast food.

"You into sharing, Flower?"

My pulse echoes in my ears. OMG! "What?"

"You asked if my girlfriend would share me—"

"If you were mine, I wouldn't share you. No way. No how."

His brow perks, matching the slant of his lips as they close around his fork full of pancake and eggs, then he bites half a strip of bacon.

Why is that so hot?

I can't look away, mesmerized by the flex in his jaw as he chews, the heat in his eyes as he watches me watching him. When he swallows, the bob of his Adam's apple has me gripping the counter, wishing it were him I was gripping.

"Daisy." He sets his fork down and wipes his mouth, then leans in, his arm coming around my shoulder, holding me steady and in place. "I'll let you in on a little secret. I don't share. I don't want to *be* shared. And if I were your man, I sure as fuck wouldn't be sharing you."

OhmyholyGrandmaJean. "G-girlfriend?" I embarrassingly sputter.

"Hmm." He unwraps his arm and returns to eating. "I don't have one, but I'd like to."

"Really?" He doesn't have a girlfriend? "The one who all the flowers are for?"

"Tell you what. Have dinner with me tonight. I'll answer all your questions and talk about you *keeping me*." He stands, his plate not even half eaten.

"You're leaving?" I don't bother to hide my disappointment or confusion.

"I'm late for my shift. I wanted to let you sleep and waited to be sure you were okay before I left." He eyes my head. "Be careful when you wash your hair. Take something for your headache. And don't worry about dressing up tonight. Nothing fancy. Wear whatever you want, and if you're too tired to go out, I can cook."

"You sure I can't keep you?" I mean, seriously.

He sets his plate on the counter and comes back around, turns me till I'm looking him in the chest, and tips my chin until our gazes lock. "Never said you can't keep me, Flower." He kisses my cheek and sets a piece of paper on the counter. "Call me if you need anything. Take it easy if you can. I'll see you at seven."

And just like that… he's gone.

It takes me a few minutes to get a steady breath. A few minutes more to finish the best breakfast I remember eating in the longest time. And I manage to wait only a few minutes more before I cave and text him with uncharacteristic boldness.

Me: *Thank you for yesterday. For this morning. And for not having a girlfriend. Have a great day.*

I work on cleaning the kitchen and nearly topple over when I see the amount of food in the refrigerator. I'll never eat all that before it goes bad. One person couldn't possibly… Maybe he intends to stay?

Maybe *he* wants to keep *me.*

God. I hope he does.

Or maybe he's used to buying groceries for a bunch of hungry firefighters.

Reid: *You're welcome. I have a girlfriend in mind. She's my wildflower.*

Oh, OhmyholyGrandmaJean. I thought firefighters were supposed to put out fires, not start them.

CHAPTER 5

SEVEN O'CLOCK CAN'T GET HERE SOON enough. I didn't want to leave, but duty calls, and it doesn't give a shit if I'm *finally* getting a chance with my girl. My co-workers don't care how amazing it felt to finally feel her in my arms as I held her all night. Granted, I was fully dressed except for my shoes and socks, but I'll take it over sleeping without her.

They don't care that I'm dragging ass because I kept checking on her to be sure she was really okay, not to mention checking on the basement to be sure it was draining, and there were no more water leaks. Old pipes tend to go at the same time.

The only people who might let it slide if I didn't show up today are my brothers. But only because they were there. They know how momentous last night was for me. It broke the ice. I was finally able to breach the barrier of simply being a regular customer to her. I don't know if that's how she saw me, but I felt stuck in that routine, unable to make the move, afraid of losing even that small weekly contact if I mess it up.

And messing it up is a high probability. I don't know much about having a girlfriend, but I'm sure willing to learn for her. She seems like a patient, forgiving woman. I hope I don't test those boundaries more than she can bear during the learning process.

I find Galant in the kitchen cleaning up breakfast, doing my job while I was taking care of Daisy. I sidle up next to him. "Thanks for last night and for today."

"Yeah, of course. How's she doing?"

I don't even try to hide my smile. "She's great."

His eyes widen. "Oh, really?"

"No. Not like that," I correct his assumption that we had sex. "I stayed over. I held her. Ensured she was really alright. Made breakfast. And asked her out. Then I texted her, calling her my girlfriend." Well, hinted I'd like her to be my girlfriend.

He wipes his hands and faces me. "That easily, huh?"

I shrug. "I don't know if she'd call the events of last night easy. But, yeah, this morning… it was effortless. She was open to it, open to the flirting and the possibility of something with me. Everything felt right… All the pieces falling into place. Finally."

"*Finally.* I'm happy for you, man. I really am." He pats my back as we enter the commons room. "It's about time."

"Couldn't agree more." I start to head out to work on the rest of my jobs for the day, but stop short. "I'll have my truck tonight, so I'll pick up your pump. Okay if I just bring it to work tomorrow?"

"Yeah, no reason to make an extra stop at my place. She know you prefer two wheels over four?"

I shake my head. "I don't know if she's ever noticed what I drive."

"Theo know she'll have to start buying her own flowers if she wants to keep up that weekly delivery you've spoiled her with?"

A laugh breaks free at the idea of not limiting myself to only seeing my Flower on Tuesdays. "Maybe I'll keep up the tradition. It makes her feel special." Theodosia is the youngest and only daughter in my parents' brood of five. She didn't get treated much like a princess growing up. She had to be tough and rowdy to keep up with four older brothers. She's only a year younger than me at twenty-three, all of us kids only a year apart—our poor mom, practically pregnant for six years running.

Galant ruminates on that a moment before saying, "I'll take it from here. You're right, we should keep it up. Theo deserves to know what it's like to be treated like a lady."

"I wouldn't take it that far. I think she's more tomboy than girl under all that hair and grease."

"Yeah, but what would you do if she didn't fix you up with the sweetest rides?"

He's right. She's magic with engines. "True. In that case, we should all be buying her flowers and chocolates."

I leave him laughing as Turner shows up at the end of our conversation, trying to figure out what we're talking about. I'll let Galant fill him in.

It's a little after lunch when I text my girl.

Me: *How you feeling? You doing okay?*

Only a few minutes pass till she responds.

Wildflower: *I'm sore but good, thanks to you and your brothers for all you did. Truly. I don't even want to think what could have happened if you didn't show up when you did.*

I shudder at the thought, hoping her employees would have come to check on her eventually. It could have been so much worse. The amount of water flooding through that pipe, barely held off by her efforts, would have kept rising, eventually hitting the electrical outlets. She would have been electrocuted, and if that didn't kill her, dropping unconscious into the water would have. She would have drowned before she regained consciousness, before the power went out and her employees finally came to check on her. Only they'd have been too late.

My entire body clenches at the thought. The possibilities of *what if*.

I make a mental note to show them the water shut-off valve and the electrical box. It's one thing to know to call a plumber or electrician, and another to get in there when the water's spraying.

Me: *I'd rather not think about it, to be honest. I'm thankful I was there.*

I had a gut feeling for a reason. It paid off. I'm glad I'm learning more and more to listen to my instincts.

Me: *You feel up to a ride tonight?*

Wildflower: *Sure. What kind of ride?*

Jesus, all kinds of dirty replies inundate my thoughts. Better not to scare her off before we even go on our first date.

Me: *On my motorcycle. It's a beautiful day. I could maybe get there by 6:30p. Dress in layers.*

Visions of buying my girl some leather riding gear and a custom-painted helmet covered in wildflowers—fire daisies, to be precise—come to mind.

Wildflower: *I'm nervous but excited.*

Me: *No need to be nervous. It's just me.*

Wildflower: *Exactly.*

Me: *Flower.*

Wildflower: *Reid.*

Me: *I got you.*

When she doesn't reply. I picture her staring at her phone having no idea how to respond. Am I too direct, too honest after all this time? I feel like we've spent the last year carefully dancing around each other, neither saying how we really feel. After seeing her the way I did last night, I much prefer the direct route—from my heart to hers. I'm praying she does too.

Wildflower: *I don't know how to respond, other than to say: I'm glad somebody does.*

Me: *Always respond with the truth, like you just did. I'll see you soon, my Wildflower.*

I tuck my phone away and get back to work, praying the firehouse doesn't get a call that'll make me late.

CHAPTER 6

I'M SEETHING BY THE TIME I HANG UP, HAVING left another scathing voicemail to my slumlord. I don't understand how someone can believe it's okay just to ignore a person. I can't help but feel, if I were a man, my landlord would be jumping to attention. But as it is, I'm the pesky young—female— flower shop owner he's perfectly comfortable ignoring for weeks on end.

The emergency of the water break is dealt with, thanks to Reid and his brothers, but there's a handful of other stuff that desperately needs his attention. I may have to seriously consider getting a lawyer. For now, it's an empty threat that dies on my tongue.

The knock at my door has my heart racing for a whole other

reason. Today was a wash with no reprieve on my nerves over seeing Reid, and then going on a date with him. I don't want to blow it, come across as needy. Though, needy is exactly how he makes me feel, especially when I open the door and his gaze is already zeroed in on me as if he'd been watching me *through* the door.

"Damn, Flower." He steps back, taking in my outfit of black jeans, boots, long-sleeve cross-body top with a deep V. The ladies do look pretty spectacular, if I do say so myself, and by his admiration, I think I did well picking my all-black ensemble. His eyes finally hit mine. "Do you have a jacket?"

"I do." I turn to grab the leather jacket Stacy loaned me.

But before I make it, he grips my hips, stopping my progress. "You're killing me, Smalls," he whispers next to my ear, fanning the bare skin of my neck and chest. "Absolutely killing me, baby."

Tingles skate along my body. It takes all I have not to lean into him, ask for his mouth, his body to replace the chill his breath left behind.

His grip tightens and releases when he steps back. When I don't move, he reaches around me, pulling the jacket off the back of the chair. "Here. Let me."

When he holds it up for me to slip into, my synapses finally start firing again. I pull my small purse over my head and shoulder, then turn, sliding my arms in the awaiting sleeves. He pulls it up, fixing the collar as I turn to face him. "There." His gaze lingers, caressing mine. "You okay? You looked stressed when you opened the door."

I shrug and snatch my phone off the counter. "I'm good."

As we head for the door, his soft grip on my wrist stops me. "Don't do that."

"Do what?"

"Pretend like nothing's wrong when something's clearly bothering you. Tell me," he urges, pulling me by the jacket till we're toe to toe.

I don't want him to think I'm asking more of him. "It's just… stuff." I shake my head and pat his chest. "Come on." I tug him toward the door, my sequoia barely moving. "Let's get this date started."

"Flower." The gruff in his voice has me stilling and staring into the depths of his tender brown eyes.

"Reid."

He sighs, stepping into me. "I want to know all your *stuff*. Good or bad, I want it all if it involves you."

"If I tell you, you have to promise not to do anything about it. Then I'd like something from you."

His eyes narrow. "I won't promise to take no action if it's something I need to act on. And whatever you want, it's yours."

He needs to stop being so nice. A girl could get used to this. A girl could *fall* for him.

"My landlord still isn't returning my calls. I'd just left a nasty message for him right before you arrived, and I wasn't feeling great about that either."

His brow quirks. "Nasty, huh?" He lifts his chin, trying to hide the slight smile tipping the corners of his lips. "Like what?"

"Don't laugh at me." I push on him and lose my balance when he doesn't budge.

He steadies me with a strong grip on my hips.

Why does that feel so good, to feel his strength, his touch, knowing he has so much more to give?

"Not making fun. Just trying to picture you being mean." He shakes his head. "I don't see it."

"Yeah, well, I can get tough when I need to." I'm not pouting. I can be tough. I just don't like to be.

He chuckles. "I'm sure you can, Flower. Now tell me. Whaddya say?"

"I told him if I didn't hear back from him immediately, if not sooner, I'd be reporting him to the Better Business Bureau and siccing my lawyer on him."

His brows rise. "You have a lawyer?"

"Nope. But he doesn't know that."

"Hmm." He guides me to the door. "And how many times have you threatened that?"

"None. I've gone from being nice, to disappointed, to stern, to angry, to threatening. Nothing seems to work. It's been weeks, and he hasn't returned a single phone call."

"I've got a friend—"

"Nope." I hold up my hand. "You promised—"

"No, I didn't. You need help. I know people." He eyes my scowl and softens. "We'll talk about it later." He opens the door for me. "Now, what is it you need from me?"

"A kiss." I start to step through, but he tugs me back inside, closing the door.

"Say that again."

CHAPTER 7

I COULDN'T HAVE HEARD HER CORRECTLY, OR if I did, I need confirmation. Pulling her back inside, I close the door and barricade her against the wall. I want to swallow her gasp with my mouth, plunder those plump lips till they're swollen and her eyes are glassy with want.

In her face, heart racing, voice tight, I take a deep breath and let it out. "Say that again."

She touches my chest, her small hands like little warmers across my pecs. I wait for her to find her words, her courage, while she's locked in my focus, her doe eyes fluttering with dark lashes I want to feel tickling my skin.

"Y-you don't have a girlfriend, right?" She looks down, but I can't have that. I need her eyes.

I tip her chin till I'm graced with her pale green gaze. "I'm staring at her."

"I'd hoped, but… OhmyholyGrandmaJean, you make me nervous. I don't want to worry *will he or won't he kiss me. Does he even want to—*"

I feed her my silent response, closing the distance, taking her mouth in a slow, barely-there kiss, parting, then pressing, teasing her bottom lip till she opens, inviting me in, and in, and in.

Do I want to kiss her? She'll never entertain that doubt again by the time I'm done consuming her mouth, drawing out her gasps, and feeding them right back to her.

Do I want to kiss her? The question should be, *Can I ever stop?*

No. That's a hell no.

Her nails bite at my skin through my t-shirt, her tongue playing with mine, teasing, urging, leaning into our tangled kiss. I knead her back, my hand slipping lower to feel the curve of her ass and lightly squeeze. Her moan has us breaking for air.

"Fuck, Flower," I pant, looming over her nose to nose. "Don't ever doubt I want to kiss you on your mouth or anywhere else you desire."

"Ohmy…"

I chuckle and grip the back of her head, granting me her eyes. "Don't filter. Not with me."

"OhmyholyGrandmaJean," she breathes across my lips, her head tilted back, nearly hitting the wall.

I don't know who that is, but my girl is cute as fuck. "You ready to go?"

Daisy visibly swallows and nods. "I don't think my legs work, though." Her bashful smile has me leaning in, stealing another quick kiss.

"I'm a firefighter. I'm trained to carry people. I got you." I lift till she wraps her legs around me, lock and shut the door, kissing her cheek as I descend the stairs. "I've always got you."

Her muffled response is buried in my neck, but I felt her shiver, her approval of my words. So far, so good. I haven't scared her off with my take-charge, no-bullshit ways.

I set her next to my bike, holding her by the waist, ensuring she's steady. "You ever been on a motorcycle, Flower?"

"No." She bites her bottom lip. Damn, there's going to be so much kissing in the not-too-distant future.

I show her the helmet I brought for her, helping her put it on, then mine as I explain, "I'll get on first, then you slide on behind me. I'll show you where to put your feet so you don't get burned."

Her eyes widen. "Okay. And I hold on to you?"

I smile. That's the best part. "Yeah, you hold on to me good and tight."

We zip up our jackets and mount my bike. Once she's settled with her feet on the pads, I pat her thigh, speaking over my shoulder, "Scoot up, right against me, arms tight around my waist." As soon as she does, I squeeze her hands. "Don't let go. If you need something, and I don't hear you, squeeze me twice, and I'll pull over. Okay?"

"Yeah, okay."

I don't miss the nervous catch in her voice. "I got you, Flower. Just lean into me and relax. Let me take you on a ride."

She nods and sinks into me, laying her head on my back. I flip my visor closed and start my girl—my *other* girl. When she purrs to life, Daisy screeches then laughs. I pat her hand. "Ready?"

"Ready."

Pulling onto the street, her grip tightens and holds. Not our signal. She's good.

Once we leave the city limits, heading toward the ocean, she relaxes, still plastered to my back but no longer tense.

As the miles pass, I itch to keep going, keeping her right where she is for as long as possible, but I also itch to get to our destination, wanting to beat the sunset, spend time together, just the two of us, and let the rest of the world fade away.

I stop at the last gas station before we go off road. "Last pit stop before we get where we're going. There's no bathroom there, so—"

"I should take advantage and go now." She hops off my bike like she's been doing it for years, handing me her helmet and un-abashedly smiling at me, fluffing up her curly brown hair. Her gaze drops to my lips before sweeping back up. "You need anything?"

Catching her around the waist, I haul her to me. "Just this." I dive in for a sweet kiss or two to reinforce my new ability to do so.

Breathless, she pulls away and turns, heading inside with a little extra sway to that gorgeous ass. I groan my approval and don't stop watching till she's inside, then top off my tank so I don't have to do it on the way home.

CHAPTER 8

R ELUCTANTLY, I PEEL MY FRONT OFF REID'S
back. I might have been getting a little warm, but I'd never
admit it or put air between us. I was scared of his bike. I'd
never been on one. Never had any desire to ride one. Now, I'm
not sure I'll ever enjoy a four-wheeled ride again.

His gaze never leaves me as I dismount, my hand sequestered
in his. His attention is powerful, heavy, making it hard to breathe
through, hard to give him space to get off his own bike. Somehow,
I manage, my hand feeling bereft without his. My lips sympathize
missing his already. Moving back, I look out over the bluff, letting the wind whip my hair, and force a cleansing breath down
my throat, filling my lungs to capacity... one, two, three times.

Feeling steadier, I turn my attention to him in awe as he lays out a blanket, set with food and drinks. He prepared. He planned. He thought of me and did this for me—for us.

He catches my gaze and does a double-take. "Hey, you okay?" He steps into me, gently running his fingers over my cheek.

There goes my breath again. I fight for another one and meet his gaze. "I'm great. Just touched you went to all this trouble."

His smile is instantaneous and painfully kissable. His brow quirks. "This is nothing." He grazes my bottom lip with his thumb. "But this mouth… is everything."

This man is going to have me swooning on every word, isn't he?

He leans in, cupping my cheek. "I need a taste, Flower."

I grip the thick wrist of the hand holding me and lift on tiptoes to press my lips to his. Soft, gentle, yet commanding, he takes over. I manage to sweep my tongue across his seam before he opens on a growl that has a tremor sweeping up my spine and him pulling me against the hard planes of his body.

Yes, ohsweetGrandmaJean, yes. I wrap around him, gripping his hair and climbing him like the giant sequoia he is. Firm hands secured on my ass and back hold me safe and sound in his arms as he kisses me hard and deep. His moans of pleasure, of reassurance, of encouragement, only fuel the fire he lit in me all those months ago.

Nearly a year of wanting this man. A year of believing he belonged to someone else. A year of thinking he didn't really see me, couldn't be looking when he'd already found another woman.

I pull back. "So," I puff over his face. "No girlfriend all this time. Every week you came to buy flowers for whom?"

"You," he growls and steals another kiss, his hand on the back of my head, not letting up, not letting go. *Take it*, I hear in my head.

Take it.

Take it.

Take it.

Our lips red and puffy, he sets me down on the blanket. I practically fall to the ground, thankfully avoiding any food. He opens a bottled water and hands it to me.

"No girlfriend. It was an excuse to see you, get to know you in a non-threatening way."

My forehead puckers. "Non-threatening?" My mind races with all the other ways he could have gotten to know me.

He shrugs and opens a water for himself. "I'm a big, overbearing guy. I wanted you to get used to me without me overwhelming you."

"Like you are now?"

Swiping at a lock of my hair, his eyes flash to mine. "This is me holding back, Daisy."

Wow. "So, what's it like when you let go?"

He chuckles and drops to his back, gazing up at the sky. "I don't know, Flower. I've never fully let go." His head lulls to the side, brooding brown eyes searching mine. "I want to with you."

"Are you always so honest?" I love it, just not used to him speaking so much.

"I'm a man of few words. I prefer them all to be true."

"I prefer it too."

"That's good. Always be straightforward and honest with me. Don't hold back."

"But you're going to hold back with me?"

"I'll give you all you can take, Wildflower."

It sounds like we're talking about more than transparent communication here. I swallow around the lump in my throat and eye the spread before us. "What did you bring?"

"Good redirect." He sits up, chuckling when he spots my blush.

It just seemed safer territory for a first date. I don't want to scare him off getting too serious, letting him know I want all his focus, all his truth, all his delicious, tantalizing kisses. I want it all. Selfishly need it. Long to be anyone's focus. Especially his.

"Hey." He sweeps my hair over my shoulder, tipping my chin. "You wanting to change the conversation is okay. It's our first date of a lifetime of dates. We've got time."

CHAPTER 9

I WOULDN'T NECESSARILY CONSIDER MYSELF A morning person. I like to sleep and laze in bed too much to be that optimistic. But there is something about getting up before dawn, when the city is barely awake, just beginning to yawn and spreading its wings.

With my cart full of my morning's take of flowers and plants, I pause, watching the sun breach the horizon, feel its heated kiss on my skin, and make a wish of a thousand wishes, silent, and only for me. Maybe one of them is coming true. Reid.

"I wondered if I'd see you today. I expecting you yesterday." Mary's scratchy voice widens my smile.

"Morning, Mary. How are you?" I take one more glance at

the sunrise and turn my focus to the kind woman before me. She owns the Flower Mart, where I get most of my supplies.

"I'm good. Missed you yesterday." She's not letting it go. I'm sure she had a plan of attack all laid out. She's been trying to set me up with one of her sons. I'm not big on blind dates. Actually, I've never been on one, and I don't intend to start now.

"I had an emergency at the store, set my week back a bit. But I'm here now." I eye my cart and catch her gaze still on me. "Do you have anything special hiding back there? Maybe some ranunculus or bleeding hearts?"

Her face lights up. She loves to talk flowers as much as I do. "I had some ranunculus come in this morning, and I haven't had time to set them out. You want to see if something catches your eye?"

She's allowing me into the inner sanctum, her goody bag. I'd be crazy to pass up an offer like that. "Is it a beautiful morning? Of course I want to see all the beauties."

Her laugh trails behind her as she leads the way. "I love your passion for flowers. I wish I could convince you to come work with me."

"If I can't catch a break with my landlord, I may have to."

"Really? Did you threaten him with the BBB and a lawyer?" She suggested it weeks ago when I mentioned I was having landlord issues.

"I did. Still nothing." I know a lot of people are falling on hard times. I'm lucky to still have a successful business. But if the place is falling apart around me, how long will it last? Especially if I have to pay for all the needed repairs. It'll eat up any profits before I know it.

"You know, my sons have quite a few contacts in this city. I'd be happy to reach out to them—"

"Let me guess, if I agree to go out with one of them?"

She laughs. "I'm not that cruel, and they're not that desperate, despite the optics of my meddling. I'd love for you to meet my youngest, but it's not a stipulation of our helping you." She bands her arm with mine as we enter the back of her warehouse. "Us businesswomen have to stick together. There's power in numbers."

"I appreciate it… Oh my, just look at them." I bend down to take a lungful of honey and orange blossom from the fragrant row of sweet peas. "I could live here."

She shakes her head, finding my love of flowers endearing. At least I hope that's what her humored gaze implies. "Come on, the ranunculus are over here. Don't get distracted."

If she only knew how distracted I am this morning. Memories of Reid dance in my head like only a giant sequoia could. I touch my lips, wondering if they're still swollen from a night of amazing, life-altering kisses, and a firefighter who wants to take me on another ride on the back of his motorcycle this weekend.

"You sure I can't convince you to give my youngest boy a shot?"

I want to say yes because this woman took me under her wing, showed me the ropes when I was just getting started, gave me deal after deal on amazing flowers to be sure I made a profit.

She's the reason my business is booming. I don't want to disappoint her. But…

"I'm seeing someone." I don't wish I wasn't seeing Reid, but I do wish I could make her happy. I never said yes to her because of Reid. The moment I met him I've held out hope that he'd be free, eventually, and then pick me as his next girl instead of coming in to pick flowers for someone—anyone—else besides me. It's crazy, yes. But waiting has paid off, and it turns out he did see me all along.

Her sweet smile fades. "I thought as much. You have a glow about you that wasn't there last week. Is he a good boy, kind, well-mannered?"

"He is." And so much more.

She motions to the plastic curtain. "They're just inside. Take what you want." She turns away. "I'll see you outside when you're ready to check out."

"Mary—"

"I'm happy for you, Daisy. You let me know if you need any help with that old fuddy duddy of a landlord. Okay?"

"Yeah, I will. Thank you."

"Don't mention it." She slips away, and my morning of sunrise and sweet-smelling flowers feels dull and underwhelming now. I've hurt her feelings, like I rejected *her* and not her *offer* of a blind date with her son, whom I'm sure is a great guy with a mom like her.

When I get back to the store, the knot of disappointing Mary still sits firmly in my stomach. I take a chance he's not busy and text Reid.

Me: *Tell me something good.*

Reid: *You.*

Me: *Funny.*

Reid: *Not being funny.*

For the millionth time today, I touch my lips and hide my smile behind the back of my hand, though nobody is even around to see it. Is it silly how his serious reply sets flutters off in my stomach? I mean, I have work to do, and all I really *want* to do is daydream about him and how it feels to be in his arms and the focus of his passion.

I set my phone aside and take a deep breath. There's more work to be done than I have hours in the day. I should get to it.

I get Mark loaded up and off for his morning deliveries before he heads to class. He'll come by after to finish up any late deliveries or anything else I may need. Stacy is covering the front of the store and doing simple arrangements in between customers. I slip out back to work on the hand-painted vases for a wedding in a few weeks. I only have five more to go. Maybe a few extra in case one breaks. It's not a huge wedding, but the bride spotted my painted vases I have out front and wanted to know if I could order more. She was ecstatic to learn I paint them myself. The vases are for each table as the centerpieces for the reception. She's going to give them as bridal party gifts, though I think she'll have more vases than attendants.

Music playing, a light breeze coming in from the back door, I lose myself in the delicate task of painting flowers, each petal and leaf positioned in such a way to match the previous vase.

A mix of roses, stock, bleeding hearts, and lilies are her selection, along with the bride and groom's names and wedding date. I pride myself on being able to offer a personal touch even some of the largest chain shops can't.

I paint the last stroke on vase number five and set it down. Movement to my left catches my attention. I nearly come off my stool when Reid steps out of the shadows.

CHAPTER 10

"I DIDN'T MEAN TO SCARE YOU."

"No. It's okay." She puffs out a breath, trying to calm the fear I set free by sneaking up on her.

"You were deep in. I didn't want to mess you up by suddenly announcing my presence."

"It's okay." She drops the paintbrush in a cup and stands to wash up.

"I didn't realize you paint too." Did she paint all the vases decorating the front of the store? I move closer, inspecting her work. The colors are soft yet bright. Painted flowers wrap around the center of the vase, her stokes covering the glass, yet leaving small gaps to allow light to penetrate, illuminating the flowers.

"It's nothing. Just something I enjoy doing more than anything else."

"They're identical." I frown at the surprise in my voice. I hope she doesn't think I'm doubting her abilities.

"That's the idea."

I come to my full height, my eyes on her watching me, studying my body as if she sees something new each time. "Do you use stencils?"

She shrugs off what's meant to be a compliment but doesn't quite sound like one. "Symmetry comes naturally, I guess. My mom used to paint," she offers, like that explains how she's so good. Maybe it does.

"Did you go to school for this?"

"No, I have a business degree."

"You're really talented." I try again to let her know I think she's remarkable.

She smiles and moves closer. "Aren't you supposed be fighting fires, rescuing cats, and helping old ladies cross the street?"

Funny. She's cute when she's sassy. "Boy Scouts handle the old lady crossings. They're pretty territorial about that."

She laughs. "Yeah, but I imagine you can hold your own."

"Always." I pull her close, resting my hands on her hips. "What's up with the text? Something upset you? You didn't respond."

She toys with her lip, frowning. "It's nothing. I was just having a blah morning."

"Daisy." She relaxes at my tone, letting out another sigh, her shoulders dropping an inch or two. "What really happened?"

"There's a lady who keeps trying to set me up with her son. She's so nice, but—" she waves at me, "—you know, I'm even less interested than I was before. I feel like I'm letting her down."

Mom. She struck again. I should have given her a heads-up that I've already closed the deal, but hearing my Flower turned down a blind date with me because she's already dating me fills my chest with a warm, welcome feeling, like she's claiming me, letting the world know she's no longer available—even if it's just my meddling mom.

"You feel bad because you want to see this guy?" I tease. "Check your options?"

Her eyes widen. "No. I feel bad because she's always so nice. She helped me get my shop up and running with endless advice and discounts on supplies. She's helped me out of more scrapes than I can remember, and I have nothing to offer her—"

"Except yourself for her son?"

"Stop. You almost sound jealous." She pushes on my chest, trying to move away, but I don't let her.

If she only knew how ridiculous it is, me being jealous over me, but somehow I am. Plus, she's so cute trying to defend against my ribbing. "Not jealous. Possessive. Maybe I need to meet this guy. Let him know you're not available."

"I doubt he even knows I exist." She rests her palms flat on my chest.

Oh, he knows. "Let me take you to lunch, make you feel better."

"I've so much to do, but maybe I could make us lunch at my place."

"Sold." I grab her hand, pulling her to the door before she can take her next breath.

"Wait." She tugs on my arm. "I need to tell Stacy."

I sweep her off her feet. "Hey, Stacy!"

She pops in from out front. "Yeah?" Her eyes turn to saucers when she spots my girl in my arms, and then she snickers.

"Daisy is fixing us lunch. You okay to man the store?"

Stacy pops a hip. "Of course. Enjoy." She turns. "Don't rush on my account, Boss."

Daisy laughs, burying her head in my neck. Not planning on rushing, except getting her upstairs.

In her tiny apartment, I set her on the kitchen counter. She looks everywhere but at me. "You probably know what I have since you bought all the groceries. What do you feel like?"

"You." I settle closer, forcing her legs apart, sliding my hands up her thighs, then waist, stopping just below her breasts, giving her a slight squeeze.

A sweet blush rises up her cheeks. "I'm serious. What do you want to eat?"

"You."

"OhmyholyGrandmaJean." She hides behind her hands. "I can't believe you said that."

Oh, Flower, if only you knew how dirty my thoughts run.

I pry her hands open, holding them captive. "The answer to every one of your questions is *you*, Flower:

"Tell you something good. *You.*

"What do I want? *You.*

"What do I want to eat? *You.*

"Who do I want to spend my time with? *You*.

"What do I want to do after work? *You*."

I release her hands and bracket her face. "I want you, Daisy, in every way a man can want a woman. You'd better get used to it, as the longer we date, my desire is only going to grow."

"Do you… I mean… Are you—"

I silence her spouting with my mouth. She needs a minute, and I've waited too long for my hello kiss. Gentle nudging has her opening, offering her mouth like the delicious meal it is. I treat it more like an appetizer than a main course. There are things to say, and getting lost in her mouth is all too enticing.

Breaking our kiss, I catch her glassy gaze. "Take a breath and ask me."

Her grip on me tightens as she takes a few deep inhales, letting them out slowly, resting her head on my chest. "Are you telling me you want to have sex?"

I smile at her directness and kiss her warm lips, just one quick press of my mouth to hers. "Yes, but not just sex."

"Right now?" She doesn't have to sound so incredulous.

Another kiss, 'cause she's too adorable. "No, Flower, I'm not rushing fucking you for our first time. When you're ready, once we do, it's going to be an all-night endeavor."

She lets out a shaking breath. "All night?"

Damn, who has she dated in the past? "Yeah. All. Night. Long." I punctuate each word with a kiss. "I'm not rushing with you."

She's lost in thought. I've overwhelmed her.

I kiss her cheek and turn to the fridge. "How about *I* make us lunch?"

"O-okay."

My Daisy is too sweet for me, but it's too late. There's no turning back.

Ready or not, Wildflower.

Here I come.

All in.

No holding back.

CHAPTER 11

THE HEAT IS NEARLY UNBEARABLE, EVEN IN all my protective gear and years of building tolerance. The back of the warehouse is engulfed in flames. Barrels of something flammable pop and sizzle, seconds before exploding.

"Damn, this whole place is going to go up like the Fourth of July," Michael huffs over the radio.

"The foreman said there are still two workers unaccounted for. Jake is bringing out a survivor who thinks the others are in the north wing." I check my gauges before radioing, "I'm going to check it out." I'd planned to meet up with another team to continue searching, but I know no one has been back here. I have that tingling feeling again. That's where they are.

"Make it quick," Red orders.

"Heading your way," Galant's cool voice fills my earpiece. "Don't move, Reid. I mean it."

"I'm already there." I don't need a babysitter.

"Wait," he barks in reply.

"Checking the first door on the left." It's only a few feet away, nearly the same as waiting for him.

"Dammit, Reid."

The room is dark and empty except for the desk and chair in the corner. I run the flashlight around the walls, floors, and corners just to be sure. "Empty."

I back out and catch the headlamp of Turner and Galant's helmets as they turn the corner.

"Told you to wait," Galant growls, acting like he's my captain or battalion chief.

Big brothers don't trump the chain of command. "Good thing I don't report to you." I point across the hall. "Check right. I'm going left."

Another office and one bathroom down, I'm about to enter the next bathroom when I hear faint cries. I tag Turner on the shoulder. He's been keeping watch in the hall as Galant and I check each room to be sure we return. "You hear that?"

We still, listening. "There." I point to the next turn in the hall. "Down there."

Galant stops me with a hand on my chest. "I'll go. You finish checking these rooms then get the hell out of here."

"They could both be in there. You'll need help." It doesn't make sense to split up and keep searching what are more than likely empty rooms when the two people we're searching for could be down the next hall as my instinct is telling me.

"Fine." He looks to Turner. "Radio it in."

Galant and I lead, moving debris and checking doors as we pass. Another explosion rocks the building. Galant throws himself over me and Turner. We crash to the ground as the wall next to us crumples and flames lash overhead. The ductwork must have caught on fire.

Quick check to be sure we're all okay, then we're on the move double-time. My heart racing and visions of my Flower drive my adrenaline, keep me going into the fire instead of racing away. I've never really considered what it would be like to have someone who cares for me, someone who might worry over me not coming home at the end of the day. I grew up with firefighters. Worry was an everyday part of life, but it also made it commonplace. My Wildflower isn't used to the fireman's way of life. I don't want her to worry, and I definitely don't want to *not* come home at the end of the day.

Before I get too lost in those unproductive thoughts, a cry for help draws us to a stop. The ceiling above the door the cry came from is engulfed in flames. "Not good." It could come down at any second.

Galant calls out, and we get a muffled response. "Stand back!"

Using the brunt of his axe, he knocks the door open and stands back, giving it a second to see if fire erupts from the room. The flames above lick at the doorway but don't grow exponentially.

"Now." With Turner behind me, we rush in. The room's ceiling is a mass of orange and red flames, whirling and sizzling above our heads. In the corner, we find a man and a woman huddled together, coughing, struggling to catch their breaths.

We each grab an arm and race through the door. We don't stop. We don't look back. We run for the exit, the building cracking and exploding behind us—around us. My brothers and I each have an arm under a survivor's arm, dragging them out.

Once outside, paramedics take over as my brothers and I move away from the warehouse, huffing and puffing like we just ran a mile, adrenaline pumping, elated we found them and made it out alive.

"You should have come out with Jake when you found the first survivor." Galant pushes me. "You don't search alone."

I know this.

I *know* this.

I hold up my hand to stop his rant. "I was right there, Galant. I couldn't leave them."

"A day will come where you're going to have to choose, and you better not die making the wrong choice." He storms off.

Turner pats my back. "He's mad because he cares."

"I know." It might have been the wrong call for me, but it was the right call for the two people we saved. The room wasn't going to stay standing much longer. Seconds can be the difference between rescuing a survivor and searching for the deceased.

Galant's not wrong, though. But it's not the idea of dying that scares me. It's the idea of never seeing my Daisy again.

My Wildflower.

Back at the firehouse, after everything is cleaned up and

reloaded, I shower and eat. But when it's time to sleep, I can't unwind, can't stop my racing thoughts of *what if*.

It's late when I call Daisy. The call goes to voicemail. I leave her a mumbling fiasco of a message and wish her goodnight. Giving up on sleep, I grab a water and head out back. The cool evening usually settles me, but there's only one thing that'll settle me tonight, and she's curled up sleeping without a care in the world.

CHAPTER 12

" ... UH... SORRY IT'S LATE. I SHOULDN'T BE
calling, chancing waking you. I just wanted to hear your
voice. See how your day was. Did you get everything done
for the wedding job? I'm off that day. Can I see you after you're
done doing whatever you need to for the wedding?" He lets out a
deep sigh. "I just wanted to hear your voice." Another sigh. "I said
that already, didn't I? Sleep tight, Flower."

When the voicemail ends, the silence feels unnatural, forced,
like I let him down by not picking up, by missing his call. I listen
to his message again, wanting to glean details of what he's not
saying, read between his words of what happened to discover
what put the heavy in his voice. He's sad. That much is obvious.

Did he call so I could cheer him up, help him through whatever got him down?

We've been seeing each other for a few weeks now. Pretty much any night he's off and some mornings when he's not. We haven't moved beyond kissing and heavy petting over clothes. We're like horny teenagers. It's fun and refreshing. I don't feel rushed to take us to the next level. But that doesn't mean I'm not dying to—not willing to.

He thinks I'm in bed. I'm glad I'm not, or I would have missed his message. I clean up the work bench so it's ready for tomorrow. I stayed late to finish orders and, as he remembered, pull all the last-minute details together for the wedding.

I stop at a late-night taco shop known as an after-party must-have for its greasy, spicy goodness. Reid's mentioned it a few times, but we've never gone together. Pulling into the firehouse, I park and hesitate getting out.

Is this a mistake?

Will he get in trouble for having visitors so late or visitors at all?

Will I wake the whole place up?

A shake of my head and the sound of his voice in his message has me braving my uncertainty. I still at the firehouse door. I don't know what the protocol is. I don't want to ring the buzzer. Maybe knock softly, see if anyone hears me.

I raise my hand—

"Flower?"

I whip around to find Reid coming around the side of the

building. "What are you doing out here?" I glance between him and the door.

"I was out back, heard a car pull in. We don't get many visitors, especially not this time of night. I was coming to see who it was, head them off before they rang the buzzer and woke everyone up."

Dang, so glad I didn't push the button.

"I, uh, brought you tacos." I hold up the bag as evidence.

"Damn." He hauls me to his chest as soon as I'm within reach. "You're a sight for sore eyes."

Relief floods me seconds before his mouth crashes against mine. *Oh my.* I've missed his lips. I've missed *him*. It's been two days of busy schedules and conflicting shifts. Soft, pillowy lips demand entrance. Relief is replaced by want the tighter he holds me, the deeper he kisses.

"How'd you know I needed you?" His breath fans my face. His hands implore me closer, which is impossible unless I crawl under his skin.

"Your voicemail. What happened?"

"We had a fire." The familiar scratch in his throat has his words playing in my head, *I just wanted to hear your voice.*

My heart skips. "Are you alright? Was it bad?"

"Later. You've got to be freezing, but I can't bring you inside. It's against regs."

"I don't have to stay." I want to, at least for a minute, but I don't want to get him in trouble. "You can just eat your tacos, and I can go."

"I don't think so." He tugs me around the side of the building, coming to a stop below a pergola with a hammock, patio table, and chairs. "Be right back."

The cool breeze makes me shiver, and I'm glad I wore my coat. I don't dare pull out a chair. I don't want to make noise to bring attention to my presence and burst this beautiful bubble.

As quick as he left, he's back, wearing a coat, with a blanket tucked under his arm and two bottles of water. He's good about drinking water and ensuring I stay hydrated.

"Here." He pulls out a chair, draping the blanket over it. "Sit. I'll cover you up."

Now that I'm secured with the blanket under me and over my shoulders, he takes the chair next to me and opens the bag of food.

"I'm sorry. They're probably cold." I should have brought a thermal bag to keep them warm.

"Doesn't matter. My girl brought me delicious food. I'm eating it."

My girl. I still. The idea of being *his* awakens butterflies in my belly.

His eyes sweep my face. If he notices my blush, he's kind enough not to point it out. "You'll eat some, won't you?"

"Yes. I haven't eaten yet."

That has *him* stilling. "Why not?"

He doesn't like it when I don't take time to eat. I keep telling him I've got enough padding to keep me going for a winter or two. He doesn't find it funny. I love that he doesn't.

"I worked late. I'm not sure how I missed your call. Maybe I was in the bathroom or getting supplies."

"I don't like you working late and then having to go out back in that dark alleyway to get to your apartment. The shop needs better lighting."

"I'll add that to the growing list I'm sure my landlord will be happy to ignore."

"Still nothing from him?"

"Not a peep."

"Hmm." His scowl deepens as he hands me napkins and tacos. "I'd like to help if you'll let me."

"At this point, I'm willing to try anything. Short of suing him, I don't know what will get his attention." I can see this becoming a long discussion, and my landlord is the last thing I want to waste more time on. "Let's table that for now and eat."

Surprisingly not soggy, the crunch of tacos is the only sound for the next few minutes as we both devour taco after taco. After four, I'm done. I sit back and pull my feet up, wrapping myself in the blanket, and duck my head to hide a yawn. It's been a long day.

I enjoy watching him eat. There something purely masculine about the cut of his jaw chewing his food, the bob of his Adam's apple when he swallows, and the swipe of his tongue to catch any stragglers on his lips. He pauses when he catches me staring. His brow quirks, but he doesn't stop. He's not embarrassed or self-conscious in the least. He takes another bite, consuming half the taco in one mouthful. How glorious it must be to be him. But there's worry in his eyes I don't remember seeing before.

I run my fingers through the side of his hair, its silky strands teasing my skin. He turns his head and kisses the inside of my wrist, the gesture so tender, my eyes prick as warmth of what can only be described as love blooms inside me. I've felt it before, niggling whispers making my pulse dance and dreams ignite of what it would be like to be loved by him.

"I'm falling," the whisper escapes before reason takes hold.

And why isn't that as scary as it should be?

He captures my hand, kissing my palm before leaning forward, holding my hand to his chest, and whispers, "I'll catch you."

Did I just admit to falling in love with him? Did he acknowledge it? Does he feel anything close to what I'm feeling?

He places our trash in the bag, balling it up and leaving it on the table, and stands, holding out his hand.

I take it, no hesitation.

He spreads the blanket across the hammock and lies down. "I need to hold you." He urges me down, lying alongside him, practically *on* him with my head on his chest, and covers us up with the other half of the blanket, wrapped like a taco. He kisses my forehead, pulling me closer. "I'm falling too."

His admission ripples along my skin. I kiss his jaw, saying in relief, "I'll catch you."

CHAPTER 13

I'VE BEEN HOLDING BACK. I SAID I WASN'T going to, but I have. I've been giving her time to settle into the idea of us before letting myself fully dare to believe… and dive in. Once we take that next step—her giving her body to me and me to her—there's no coming back. There's no undo. No brain wipe. No cooling-off period. It's a five-alarm fire, and it only gets hotter from there.

The other night she came to check on me after my rambling voicemail touched me more than she knows. She didn't know any details, just heard something in my voice and knew I needed to see her, hold her, breathe the same air as her.

I held her late into the night, the hammock softly swaying

in the night's breeze. I didn't tell her about the fire. I didn't want to scare her, or give her any reason to doubt my safety. I made a silent promise to never be so reckless again. I've no intention of missing out on a single day with her in my life, or more specifically, me in hers. I'm looking toward our future, and it doesn't involve me dying in a fire. God willing.

But it does leave a lingering question: Do I love what I do enough to put that burden on her?

I'm a firefighter because my brothers, father, and grandfather were all firemen. It was the natural course for my life to go. I didn't really have any other interests that screamed for me to take an alternate route, find a different vocation. It wasn't my dream job, but nothing was, and because I showed an aptitude, I followed my brothers. I took the easy path instead of figuring out what it is I truly love. But I'm starting to see it's my Flower. She holds my heart, and though she is amazing, she's not a career path.

My sister's lucky in that regard. She could have become a firefighter, but *she* has a calling, a deep-set instinct and talent for all thing mechanical, particularly cars and motorcycles. She was tinkering in Dad's garage before she could form full sentences, definitely before she could read. Honestly, I don't remember that far back. I'm only a year older than her. I was probably out back eating dog food and playing catch with said dog. I never claimed to be the sharpest tool in the shed, but I am the biggest, at least in my family.

Theo stands at the garage entrance as I park my bike, wiping off her hands, a big grin on her face, her dark hair secured back with a bandana. She looked pretty much the same when she was four, a total tomboy, but she's pretty cute in her coveralls and a grease stain on her cheek, happy and content.

"Hey." I nod as I take off my helmet.

"Your girl sounds like she needs a tune-up." She frowns, staring lasers into my Harley like she can figure it out from that distance without even laying a finger on her. Damn, she probably can.

"You just did a tune-up. She sounds fine." She purrs nice and low, exactly how I like it.

My brat of a sister turns, shrugging, heading inside. "Your loss. Don't come cryin' to me when she breaks down on you."

I follow, grabbing the lunch I brought. "She's not breaking down. You'd never let that happen."

"True that." She eyes the bag in my hand. "Whaddya bring?"

"Subs. You grab drinks. Meet you in back." I leave her to wash her hands, again. She may enjoy getting her hands dirty, greasy, but she's fastidious about cleaning up, especially prior to eating.

"Lenny," I greet one of the other mechanics before slipping out the back door.

"Hey, Reid. How's it hanging?"

Heavy and in need of my woman. "None of your damn business." He's a bit of a twat. Has a thing for Theodosia, has for as long as I can remember. His pops owns the place, making Lenny believe he has more power than he does. I'll have to watch what I say, knowing he'll be lurking around, listening. Total dickweed.

"I have to admit, I was a bit skeptical when Galant started showing up with flowers instead of you." Theo waves off my glower. "Not about the flowers, about you and your girl."

That's not any better. "Doubts?"

"Because, dumbass, she hasn't bit in a year, and now all of a sudden you're... together. It doesn't make sense."

"Doesn't have to, to you. *We* get it." I unwrap my sub and take a bite. By the lines on her forehead, she's still confused. "You're on the outside looking in, Theo. You're not in my heart or hers where it makes complete sense."

"Wow. That's kinda deep." She laughs, giving up and digging into her lunch. "When do I meet her?"

"Never."

"Come on, Reid. You know I give you a hard time because I care," she reasons.

"Yep, but I won't subject her to Judgy McJudgyPants."

"Cute." She points a finger. "I'm not judgy. I'm a concerned sister. That's all. Who am I to judge about life choices? I'm a female mechanic who babies her tools more than her hair."

A comfortable silence surrounds us as we eat, lost in our thoughts. When we finish, I collect our trash, toss it in the dumpster and wait for her to walk with me to my bike. She's too skinny. Her all-consuming focus when she works reminds me of Daisy. Both of them get lost in their work and forget to eat.

Theo needs a man in her life to fatten her up, remind her to eat and drink, maybe even inspire her to lose the coveralls every now and again. Another thing she has in common with my girl, except Daisy's overalls don't hide her body. They only have straps over the shoulders and open sides. She's cute as fuck in them. Theo's coveralls are as the word implies, full-bodied to protect the clothing beneath.

I can't help but wonder if Theo wears them more often than

not, even when she's not working, to protect herself from the world. If she doesn't try, she can't be hurt or disappointed.

With that thought I stop short. "You doing okay?" I feel guilty for not bringing her flowers every Tuesday since I'm dating Daisy now. Even though it was an excuse to see Daisy, it was an opportunity to spend a few minutes with Theo too. It couldn't have felt nice for that to go away so suddenly.

"Yeah, I'm good. Maybe not I've-got-a-new-love good, but I'm okay. Work is good."

"Work is always good."

"True that."

"You'd like her," I throw out before I can change my mind. I want them to be friends. I was kinda kidding about them not meeting. But kinda not. I don't want anyone giving my Flower a hard time. If we can avoid it, we will, even if it's my own family.

"Mom loves her. She must be ecstatic."

"She doesn't know. Don't tell her," I warn. I've told my brothers the same.

Her eyebrows nearly disappear under her bangs. "Mom's going to be pissed you didn't tell her."

"She'll understand. I need this time with Daisy, just the two of us. I don't want Mom fawning all over her more than she already does, scaring my girl off."

"And Daisy won't tell her? Doesn't she see Mom every week at the Flower Mart?"

"Daisy doesn't know Mary is my mom."

"Whoa… wait. You didn't tell her?"

"No." I never asked Mom to pursue Daisy for me. In fact,

I asked her not to. But the woman won't listen. By the time I found out...

"Dude. You're in a world of hurt if you don't tell her before she finds out."

"She won't care."

"Then why haven't you told her?"

Shit. I didn't want to drop that news on Daisy just when we started to make progress. Was that the wrong decision?

"Reid. Seriously. Tell. Her."

"Yeah, yeah." I will. But when?

A quick hug and a kiss on the cheek, and I'm off. I've got things to do before tonight's date with Daisy after she finishes the wedding job.

Theo's concern over Daisy not knowing who my mom is lingers, lying like rocks in my gut.

I need to tell her. It's that simple.

CHAPTER 14

THE FLOWERS FOR THE WEDDING WERE A success, and the delivery went off without a hitch. I was able to get in the chapel early to set up, left the bouquets and boutonnieres for the bridal party, and corsages and boutonnieres for the parents with the wedding planner, then rushed over to the reception location to set up the centerpieces. The chapel flowers would be donated to the church, so there was no need for me to return to the church to transport them to the reception, as I'd planned. That was a welcome surprise.

I make it back to the shop as Stacy is closing up. Just a quick *hello, goodbye, see you tomorrow* before I'm in my apartment, taking a moment to breathe.

I'm two hours early. I call Reid. Maybe he'll want to come over now.

He's breathing heavily when he answers, "Hey, everything okay?"

"Yeah, I'm home. Job is done. I—"

"On my way," he's quick to reply.

I laugh, delighting in his exuberance. "I'm going to jump in the shower—"

"Wait for me."

"—I… What?"

"I've been working out. I need a shower. Wait for me." The rasp in his voice weakens my knees. He wants me. He's never hidden that. But—

"You want to shower with me?"

"If you're not ready, I can shower after you—"

"No… I'm… It's just." I sigh my exasperation. "Will you ever stop surprising me?"

"God, I hope not, Flower. I'll see you shortly."

Wait for me.

Yeah, totally waiting. But I will brush my teeth.

I step out of my truck and stop. The sight of my girl standing at the top of her stairs waiting for me has my heart skipping a beat. She's in a black dress, feet bare, hair wavy around her shoulders and back.

"You're a sight, Flower."

Her sweet smile plays in her eyes. "Is that a good thing?"

I grab the bags from the back seat. "It's a very good thing."

Before she can consider it further, I'm bounding up the stairs. I hate that she lives above her shop but am happy as hell to see her.

Inside, I bypass her to put away what needs to be in the refrigerator and leave the rest on the counter. Returning, I sweep her in my arms. "Shower?"

Her blush is an aphrodisiac, not that I need any help. I've been hard since she said the word *shower*. Actually, it was her picture popping up on my phone screen when she called that started it all.

"Yes, please."

Damn, so polite.

In her bedroom, I give her a second to hang up her dress that would've ended up on the bathroom floor if she hadn't asked so nicely. Plus, now she's just in her bra and panties. Win-win.

I pull off my sweaty t-shirt and joggers, leaving me in my boxer briefs. Her heated appraisal burns along my chest as I walk her backward to the bathroom in the hall, barely touching her, knowing the second I do, it's going to be a roaring inferno. There are things to say before we get carried away.

Sinking my fingers into her hair at her nape, I draw her adoring gaze to mine. "Anything that happens or doesn't happen is up to you, Daisy." Her lips part as she gives a slight nod. That mouth has starred in too many fantasies to count, but this body, curved and plump in all the best ways, damn, gonna have me a feast. "Tell me what you want." *Tell me I can have you.*

Her mouth opens and closes, only her labored breaths making a sound. I love how she gets tongue-tied, her mind working a million miles a minute, her body unable to express beyond its visceral reactions. "You," she manages.

Thank God. "You've got me." With just the tips of my fingers, I trace the curve of her jaw, down her neck, and along her shoulders, dipping to glide over the swell of her breasts. Goosebumps erupt, and my cock tries to break free of my underwear.

In kind, my tactile girl runs her hands along my abdomen and chest, tracing the lines and ridges of my muscles that bunch and flex in response, driving me crazy.

I kiss along her jaw, nibbling her earlobe before asking, "Can I undress you?"

"Please," she releases in a drawn-out sigh.

Edging her back to rest against the bathroom counter, I leave her for a moment to turn on the shower. She mentioned once it takes a while to warm up. So while it does, I'll heat things up on my own.

My girl's gone nervous, biting her lip, worry rimming her eyes.

"What's wrong?" I cup her cheek.

"Should we have *the talk?*"

My brow bunches. Which one? There are so many. "The I-love-you talk?"

"Oh." Her eyes widen, then crinkle at the corners with her

smile. "I was thinking the it's-been-awhile-I'm-clear-I'm-on-birth-control talk. But yours... wow."

I tease her mouth with mine and run my hands along her sides, coming up her back to unhook her bra, dragging it down her shoulders and watching as her luscious breasts come into view. "All my tests are negative, Flower. It's been a *long* while for me." *Like over-a-year while. Like I might-just-come-as-soon-as-I-touch-your-beauties while.* Dipping low, I pick her up by the ass and stifle her laugh with a flick of my tongue across her rosy peaks.

"Oh God." She grips the back of my head and wraps her legs around me.

I take that as a good sign and continue my exploration, licking, biting, and sucking one breast before moving on to the other. Pushing her against the wall, I raise her higher so my mouth can go lower. But she squirms out of my grasp before I reach the promised land. With a groan of disapproval, I help her down before she hurts herself.

"Shower." She slips her panties off and steps in the tub, leaving the curtain open, inviting me to follow.

Not wanting to leave her invitation unanswered, I drop my boxer briefs and settle in behind her, wishing we were at my place where the shower's much larger and accommodates my size. I steal a kiss as soon as she turns. Her moan of approval has me reaching between her legs.

"Sweet Jes—"

I eat up her exclamation, claiming her mouth as I slip a finger inside her.

Hot and wet, she rocks against me, asking, "More."

"Everything," I whisper into our kiss and add a finger.

When she grips my cock, her wet hand rough and needy, my knees nearly give. It's been too fucking long since anyone's touched me. But if she keeps up this pace, I'll come before I intend to. "Flower," I warn.

"Take the edge off," she breathes across my lips and places her foot on the edge of the tub, giving me room to really go to work on her as her grip on me tightens and her hips force my fingers deeper.

"Fuck." I'll make it up to her, love her good and slow next time. But for now, I fuck her fist and ravage her mouth as she rides my fingers so fucking good. My Wildflower is all feral instinct. She may be short of words, but her body knows exactly what it wants, and it makes me ravenous, insatiable, about to come all over her stomach and breasts.

When she gives up holding on to my arm for support, trusting I won't let her fall, the hand not working my cock plays with my balls and taint, begging me, "Give it to me."

Not about to go off on my own, I corral her against the cool tiles, draping her leg over my raised knee, and slide my other hand behind her, lowering to tease her back entrance as I finger fuck her pussy.

"Ohmyholy..." She clenches and shakes, and her whole body goes rigid, her hand on my cock squeezing so hard, I nearly lose sight as I come with her, ribbons of cum flowing between us, her pussy drenching my fingers.

"Reid," she sighs into my chest, still stroking my cock, drawing tremors and waves of pleasure from me.

I kiss her wet hair, letting my truth free as I release a ragged breath, "I love you, Daisy."

"Reid." Her doe eyes lock on me, glistening with emotions. "I love you too."

CHAPTER 15

SOMETHING STIRS ME FROM SLEEP, AND IT'S not the giant sequoia next to me, dwarfing my queen bed. He's out cold. No wonder. I think he ate a couple pounds of pasta. Granted, it was delicious. I've always loved a hearty meat sauce. My man can cook.

I glance at the clock. It's after two in the morning, hours before I need to get up for work. Then I hear it, glass breaking, and almost like a sizzling, cracking noise. I sit up, my gaze flying to the bedroom door that's glowing.

Is that… smoke?

"Oh, my God. Reid!" I shake him, practically on top of him before he opens his eyes.

"Flower?" He scowls then comes upright, gripping my arms to keep me in place, sniffing the air. "Fire."

I point to the door. "I think my apartment's on fire." My voice and chin tremble.

He jumps out of bed, picking up his phone. "Get dressed."

His calm doesn't help me find mine. But I do manage to throw on some clothes, eyeing him as he moves around the room dressing and assessing. He doesn't open the bedroom door. He doesn't even touch it. He backs away, glances at me, grabs the sheet from the bed, stuffs it in the crack at the bottom, and heads for my closet. I don't miss his quick look to the one window in the room.

Should I open it?

I slip on my tennis shoes left at the end of my bed, grab my phone and computer, trying to remember what you're supposed to do in a fire.

Drop and roll.

No, that's if you're *on* fire.

He comes back seconds later with my duffel full to bursting with clothes. "Don't open the window. Try to stay calm, stay low. Firetrucks are on their way."

He called 9-1-1. Thank God one of us is thinking straight.

"Grab anything in here irreplaceable." He opens my dresser drawers and starts stuffing bras and panties into the duffel.

Oh my god, we're going to die.

"Hey." He drops the bag on the bed, stuffs my laptop and phone in and zips it up before gripping my shoulders. "You're going to be okay. They'll be here before the fire makes it through the door."

I look at the floor, images of flames licking at my feet. "The shop."

"Its fire-proof barrier will keep the fire at bay long enough to get out."

"But my apartment—"

His grip tightens as he bends till we're eye to eye. "We don't know where it started or what's on fire. All I know is there's fire on the other side of that door, and there's no escape that way."

"So, after all this, after last night. This is how we die?" I sob into his neck. We've barely even started. This can't be how we end.

He swipes at my tears, brackets my face and kisses me soundly. "No. This is not how you die."

I take a quivered breath and nearly choke when I realize what he said. "Not how *I* die? *I* die?"

He gets us to the floor, dampens a t-shirt with my water from the nightstand and ties it around my head, covering my nose and mouth. He does the same with the water from his side. "*We're* not dying."

There's something he's not saying. He keeps glancing at the door.

"Reid?"

He doesn't answer, he just pulls me into him. "I love you, my Wildflower."

I sob harder, gripping his shirt, burying my face in his neck.

We haven't even made love yet.

"Is this where we die?"

"No," he whispers into my ear. We're moving. Then I feel a

cool breeze and fresh air. I'm on something hard. "This is where you start the rest of your life."

"Reid?" Panic hits like a shot to the gut when he pulls away and I'm on the outside looking into my smoky apartment.

"Don't move, Daisy." He grabs my bag and tosses it out the window. "I don't know how sturdy that grate is, but it should hold till the trucks get here."

"Reid?" It's not even a balcony. It's a false balcony for aesthetics. It shakes when I reach for him.

"Don't move, baby." He pulls back, his hand on the window's rim. "I have to close the window to keep the fire at bay."

"No. Don't—"

"I love you, Daisy." His eyes glistening with unshed tears, he lowers the window.

"Reid, please."

I hear the click of the lock.

"Reid!"

His palm presses against the window. "Don't move, baby." A single tear slides down his cheek a second before he disappears.

"Reid!"

THE END

Continue Reid and Daisy's story in WILDFIRE, *WILD Duet* Book two.

ACKNOWLEDGMENTS

Thank you to all the first responders who put their lives on the line every day for people they don't even know. You are truly the bravest, the best of all of us. Thanks to you and your families who support and love you.

To my sweet family who supports me endlessly. Thank you a million times over.

Thank you to my DIVAs. Your support and love of my books and writing journey mean more than you can ever know.

To all my author friends and the book community at large, thank you for your kinship, support, and camaraderie.

Thank you to my editors, Tamara and Krista, and my PA, Ashley, for making me look like I know what I'm doing.

And last, but definitely not least, to my steady readers, I thank you for buying my books, reading my stories, and coming back for more. It still amazes me I get to do this for a living, and you are the reason why. I am blessed because of you.

Don't stop. Keep reading! And don't forget to leave a review.

Blessings, Dana

ABOUT THE AUTHOR

D.M. Davis is a Contemporary and New Adult Romance Author.

She is a Texas native, wife, and mother. Her background is Project Management, technical writing, and application development. D.M. has been a lifelong reader and wrote poetry in her early life, but has found her true passion in writing about love and the intricate relationships between men and women.

She writes of broken hearts and second chances, of dreamers looking for more than they have and daring to reach for it.

D.M. believes it is never too late to make a change in your own life, to become the person you always wanted to be, but were afraid you were not worth the effort.

You are worth it. Take a chance on you. You never know what's possible if you don't try. Believe in yourself as you believe in others, and see what life has to offer.

Please visit her website, https://dmckdavis.com, for more details, and keep in touch by signing up for her newsletter, and joining her on Facebook, Instagram, Twitter, and Tiktok.

ADDITIONAL BOOKS BY
D.M. DAVIS

UNTIL YOU SERIES
Book 1—Until You Set Me Free
Book 2—Until You Are Mine
Book 3—Until You Say I Do
Book 3.5—Until You eBook Boxset
Book 4—Until You Believe
Book 5—Until You Forgive
Book 6—Until You Save Me

FINDING GRACE SERIES
Book 1—The Road to Redemption

BLACK OPS MMA SERIES
Book 1—No Mercy
Book 2—Rowdy
Book 3—Captain
Book 4—Cowboy
Book 5—Mustang

ASHFORD FAMILY SERIES

WILD Duet
Book 1—WILDFLOWER
Book 2—WILDFIRE

STANDALONES
Warm Me Softly
Doctor Heartbreak
Vegas Storm
Wicked Storm
(part of the Wicked Games Anthology)

STALK ME

Visit www.dmckdavis.com for more details about my books.

Keep in touch by signing up for my Newsletter.
Connect on social media: Reader's Group, Facebook,
Instagram, Twitter, TikTok
Follow me: Book Bub, Goodreads